Clare
the Caring
Fairy

To Zara and Naomi

Special thanks to Rachel Elliot

10 9 8 7 6 5 4 3 2 1   17 18 19 20 21

Printed in the U.S.A.   40
First edition, July 2017

Clare
the Caring Fairy

by Daisy Meadows

SCHOLASTIC INC.

The Fairyland Palace

Stage

Palace Gardens

Rainspell Pa

Tennis Court & Clubhouse

TENNIS

Sunny Days B & B

Rainspell Beach

Jack Frost's
Ice Castle

Rainspell
Island

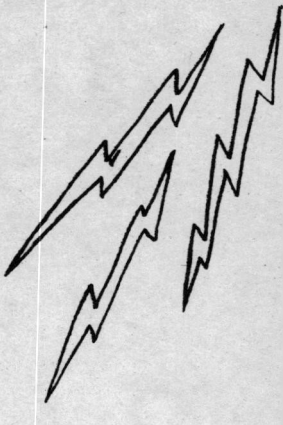

The Friendship Fairies like big smiles.
They want to spread good cheer for miles.
Those pests want people to connect,
And treat one another with respect.

I don't agree! I just don't care!
I want them all to feel despair.
And when their charms belong to me,
Each friend will be an enemy!

Contents

The Last Day

It was a beautiful summer's afternoon on Rainspell Island. Rachel Walker shut the door of the Sunny Days Bed & Breakfast behind her and skipped down the steps. Her best friend, Kirsty Tate, was waiting for her on the path, and their parents had already started walking toward the park.

"I'm really looking forward to this barbecue," said Rachel. "I'm starving!"

"I think the hot weather makes us hungrier than usual," said Kirsty with a grin. "Just *thinking* about burgers is making my stomach rumble!"

Rachel laughed and reached out to hold Kirsty's hand.

"This has been one of the best trips ever," she said as they hurried to catch up with their parents. "I can't believe that we're going home tomorrow."

"Vacations on Rainspell always go too fast," said Kirsty.

The two girls shared a secret smile. Rainspell Island was the place where they had met and become best friends, and where they had had their first adventures with the fairies.

"It's a great idea to celebrate the last day of the Summer Friends Camp with a barbecue," said Mr. Walker with a twinkle in his eye. "I love barbecues!"

At the start of their vacation, the girls had joined the Summer Friends Camp, a day camp for children who were staying on the island on vacation. Now that they had reached the end of their stay, it was time to say good-bye to all of their new friends.

"It actually has been harder to make friends than I thought it would be," Kirsty said to Rachel.

"I agree," Rachel replied. "It's all because of mean Jack Frost and his goblins. They've caused a lot of trouble."

Walking a short distance behind their parents, the girls talked quietly about the adventures they had been sharing with the Friendship Fairies over the last few days.

"It's been nonstop magic since the day we arrived," Kirsty remembered. "Esther the Kindness Fairy whisked us off to Fairyland for a tea party with her and the other Friendship Fairies."

"It was wonderful until Jack Frost turned up," Rachel added.

Jack Frost and his goblins had sneakily stolen the fairies' magical objects while no one was looking. He wanted to use them to get lots of friends that he could boss around. And, as long as he had the magical objects, friendships in the human and fairy worlds would suffer.

"Jack Frost loves trying to ruin everyone's fun," said Kirsty. "This time he's made it really hard for friends to get along. Even Jen and Ginny have argued a few times."

Jen and Ginny were the teenage best friends who ran the Summer Friends Camp.

"Thank goodness that Florence the Friendship Fairy cast a 'Friends through Thick and Thin' spell on our friendship bracelets," said Rachel. "I can't imagine ever fighting with you. It would be horrible!"

Kirsty smiled, but she still looked anxious. Ahead, her parents were laughing with Rachel's parents. Even their friendships would be ruined if Jack Frost could not be stopped.

"Florence said that the magical bracelets won't hold out for long if the fairies don't get their objects back quickly," she said worriedly. "And there is still one missing—Clare the Caring

Fairy's magical mood ring."

"We have a whole day left to find it," said Rachel. "We've already found the other three objects—I'm sure we can find it if we try our best."

"We have to," said Kirsty. "Without it, the Summer Friends Camp barbecue will be a disaster, and friendships everywhere will be destroyed!"

Barbecue Bickering

The girls followed their parents into
Rainspell Park and saw Heather the
ice cream seller. She usually sold her ice
cream in the town, but today she had set
up a little stand next to the gravel path
that ran around the park.

"She must think the park is going to get really busy because of the barbecue," said Rachel with a smile.

They both liked Heather. She was always kind and happy, and she seemed to really love her work.

"Selling ice cream must be one of the best jobs in the world," said Kirsty as they waved to Heather. "Just imagine being able to eat as much ice cream as you want!"

"I think you'd get sick of it pretty quickly," said Mrs. Walker, overhearing their conversation.

The girls looked at each other and laughed.

"Never!" they said at the same time.

The barbecue had been set up beside the tent where the camp was based. There was already a big crowd of people there, and the delicious aroma of grilled food wafted over toward them.

"There's Lara!" said Kirsty, spotting one of their new friends from the camp.

"Hello, Lara!" called Rachel, walking toward her.

Lara waved at them. She was carrying an ice cream cone from Heather's stand. As Rachel and Kirsty reached her, Oscar, another friend from the camp, bumped into Lara. Her ice cream was knocked out of the cone and fell to the ground.

"Oh no, look what you did!" Lara cried out.

"You ruined my ice cream! I only had one lick of it. You should look where you're going, clumsy!"

"I don't care," said Oscar with a shrug. "You should have been looking where you were going."

Lara stormed off, and Rachel and Kirsty exchanged a knowing look. Oscar and Lara were not usually bad-tempered, but today they didn't seem to care about anyone.

"I know exactly why they are being so mean," said Rachel in a low voice.

"Jack Frost still has the mood ring, so people have stopped caring about one another's feelings."

They walked closer to the barbecue and saw a nice seating area made from long, thick logs. Several of the other children from the Summer Friends Camp were there, but they didn't look very happy. They all had their arms crossed, and they were arguing in loud, angry voices about who should sit where. Suddenly, there was a crash and a splash. Eric had kicked his soccer ball into some drinks on a table and knocked them all to the ground.

"The drinks!" exclaimed an elderly lady. "You should be more careful, young man!"

Eric just smirked at her.

"Why should I?" he asked. "It's not my problem."

He kicked the ball again, and it crashed into the log seats and sent some of them tumbling down.

"What a rude little boy," said the elderly lady.

The girls felt very embarrassed. They knew that Eric wasn't usually rude at all.

"Things are getting worse," Kirsty whispered. "If we don't find the mood ring soon, Florence's magic might start to wear off and we might start not caring as much about each other's feelings."

The best friends looked at each other in dismay, and then hooked their little fingers together.

"We won't let that happen," said Rachel in a fierce voice. "We will find a way to stop Jack Frost!"

They went to find their parents, who were standing in the busy line for the barbecue. All the adults looked irritated, and a few of them were pushing others out of the way to try to jump ahead in the line. As the girls watched, a couple of men were nudged aside and Mr. Walker elbowed his way through the crowd. He had a burger clutched in his hand.

"I got one!" he shouted. "It's the very last one, and it's all mine!"

Kirsty, Rachel, and the other parents all stared at him in astonishment.

"What about burgers for the rest of us?" asked Mrs. Walker in a surprised voice.

Mr. Walker just shrugged as if he didn't care, and took a big bite of the burger.

"Dad?" asked Rachel in a whisper. "This isn't like you!"

But her dad took no notice. He was usually kind and thoughtful, but right then he seemed like a completely different person. Rachel turned to Kirsty, her eyes brimming with tears.

"What are we going to do?" she cried.

Mystery VIP

Kirsty gave Rachel a hug.

"Come on," she said. "This is all because of Jack Frost, and we *will* find the last magical object and stop him. Let's go say hello to Jen and Ginny, and then try to decide what to do."

But when they walked up to Jen and Ginny, the teenagers were in the middle of a big argument.

"I don't want to give the silly speech," Jen was saying. "What's the point of it, anyway?"

"What speech?" asked Rachel.

Jen and Ginny glanced at her, but they didn't even smile.

"We've written this speech about the Summer Friends Camp," said Ginny. "All about how successful it's been and how much fun we've all had. Blah, blah, blah."

"*You* can give the speech," Jen went on, glaring at Ginny.

"I don't care about the camp or the speech," Ginny snapped back. "You should do it."

They both crossed their arms and turned their backs on each other.

Rachel and Kirsty exchanged a worried look.

"Everyone is acting like they don't care about anyone else," said Rachel, feeling a lump in her throat as she thought about her dad.

"Or about any*thing* else," said Kirsty. "And it's all because of Jack Frost and his goblins."

Jen and Ginny marched off in opposite directions, and Rachel sank down on a nearby log and sighed. "I'm starting to worry that Jack Frost might really beat us this time," she said in a gloomy voice.

Suddenly, something beside the log caught her eye. It was a small watercooler, and it was glowing. Rachel jumped to her feet.

"Kirsty!" she cried. "That's magic!"

The girls kneeled down beside the little watercooler and opened the lid together. Out fluttered Clare the Caring Fairy, shivering a little.

"Hello!" she said in a bright voice, rubbing her hands together. "Thanks for letting me out—it's so chilly in there!"

She was wearing a romper covered in red roses, a sky-blue jacket, and a pair of brown ankle boots. Her gleaming auburn hair hung loosely to her shoulders.

"Hello, Clare," said Kirsty, feeling excited to see the last of the Friendship Fairies. "You'll warm up soon—it's another hot day here on Rainspell."

Rachel let out a sigh and Clare looked around at the angry faces of the people at the barbecue. A frown creased her forehead.

"It might be a warm day, but the mood

here looks as cold as ice," she said.

"Everyone is grumpy with one another," said Rachel. "They just want everything their own way."

"I have to get my magical mood ring back from Jack Frost and the goblins," said Clare. "It's the only way to make sure that people care about one another again. Please, girls, will you help me?"

"Of course!" said Kirsty and Rachel together.

"Where should we start looking?" asked Kirsty, glancing around and seeing that the crowd of people had started waving and pointing at someone. "Oh, someone very special must have arrived!"

Rachel looked over, too, and saw that Jen and Ginny were going to get a table and chair.

"He has to be able to sit and eat in comfort," she heard Ginny say to Jen.

A man scurried over to the crowd with an umbrella.

"Are you feeling too hot?" he called out, shoving people aside. "This will shade you from the sun!"

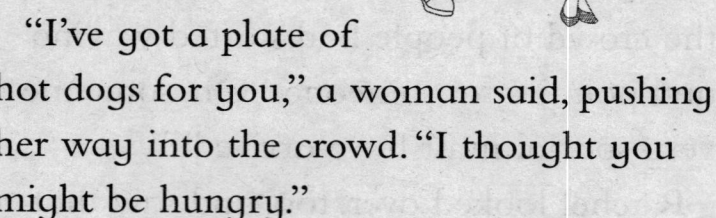

"I've got a plate of hot dogs for you," a woman said, pushing her way into the crowd. "I thought you might be hungry."

"Who *is* this amazing visitor?" asked Kirsty in astonishment.

"Cushions!" voices were calling out. "How is he feeling? Here's a footstool! Let *me* care for him!"

"Can we do anything to make you feel happier?" the girls heard Ginny asking.

"Why does everyone care about this visitor so much?" asked Rachel. "He must be someone very special to make all these people fuss over him and his feelings."

"Yes," said Kirsty, frowning. "It's even stranger when you think about how uncaring they've all been to one another. Who could he be?"

But the crowd was tightly packed around the mystery visitor, and the girls couldn't see anything.

"We have to find out who he is," said Rachel. "But *how*?"

Tempting Jack Frost

"Clare, can you turn us into fairies?" Kirsty asked in an urgent voice. "If we fly overhead, we should be able to see the visitor and find out what's going on."

Clare fluttered up and gently rested her wand against Rachel's golden hair.

Magical sparkles twinkled among her curls as fairy dust sprinkled down over her shoulders. She shrank to fairy size as Clare fluttered over to Kirsty's shoulder and cast the same spell on her. The girls smiled at each other as they spread their wings and flew up into the sky beside Clare. It was always exciting to become a fairy—even if it wasn't for a happy reason.

"Keep out of sight in the tree branches," said Clare.

From among the leafy branches, the three fairies gazed down at the crowd gathered around the mysterious visitor. Kirsty gave a gasp of shock when she saw

him. He had a long beard and a long nose,
and he was dressed in a glittery ice-blue
polo shirt and shorts. There were even
glittery blue sandals on his big
blue feet.

"It's Jack Frost!" Rachel cried out. "Why is he here in the human world? I thought he'd be in his Ice Castle, trying to keep the magical mood ring away from Clare."

"It looks like he's trying to make new friends that he can boss around," said Kirsty. "And I think he's succeeding."

All around him, grown-ups and children were fetching and carrying, bowing, and doing everything he said.

"Let's get closer," said Clare. "Maybe we can somehow stop him from bossing everyone around."

Staying high above everyone, they fluttered nearer. Clare let out a squeak of surprise and pointed at Jack's hand. A beautiful ring was glimmering on his finger—a ring that seemed to change

color every time it
moved.

"My
magical mood
ring!" Clare
exclaimed.
"We've found it—
but how are we going
to get it back?"

There were too many people around Jack
Frost—someone would be sure to spot them
if they flew down to him there. Rachel
glanced around and spotted a straggly
line next to Heather's ice cream stand.

"I have an idea," she said. "If we can
get Jack Frost thinking about ice cream,
maybe he will send some of these people
to bring him some, and we'll have a
chance to get the ring."

The fairies perched on a branch as close to Jack as they could get. There were too many people nearby to be able to get right behind him, but they were near enough for him to hear them if they spoke loudly enough.

"Heather makes the most delicious ice cream I've ever tasted," said Rachel.

"Mmm, it's so good," said Kirsty. "The perfect thing for such a hot day."

"The strawberry flavor tastes as juicy as real strawberries," Clare added. "It's so refreshing."

They were watching Jack Frost as they talked, and they saw him lick his lips.

"What else can we do to make you comfortable?" called a voice from the crowd.

"Bring me ice cream," Jack Frost said immediately. "A yummy ice cream cone—a strawberry one. Now!"

The crowd around him turned and raced off across the park toward Heather's stand. Jack Frost let out a happy sigh and leaned back against the cushions, his hands clasped across his tummy. The sun beat down on his face and his eyes flickered and then closed. A tiny snore escaped his lips.

"This is our chance," Kirsty whispered. "Let's swoop down and try to slip the ring off his finger."

"What if he wakes up?" asked Clare, biting her lip.

"We have to risk it," said Rachel, squeezing Clare's hand. "Don't be scared—we'll all be together!"

The fairies flew down and hovered beside Jack Frost's hands. The finger wearing the mood ring was on top.

"All we have to do is slide it off without waking him up," Kirsty whispered. "Come on, we can do it!"

They each got a grip on the ring and started to pull as slowly as they could. Luckily, the ring was a little loose on his bony finger. It was possible to move it along without brushing against his skin. They just had to be very careful, and very slow.

But suddenly, there was a rumbling sound in Jack Frost's chest. Then he let out a loud burp and opened his eyes.

"Fairies!" he exclaimed. "Get away from me!"

He swatted at them with his hands. Clare darted backward, but Rachel and Kirsty crossed their arms and hovered just out of his reach.

"You are causing big problems for everyone," Rachel said. "Give Clare her ring and let everything go back to normal."

"No!" Jack Frost snapped.

He jumped up and ran away from them.

"Quick, follow him!" Kirsty cried. "We can't let that ring out of our sight!"

True Friendship

Kirsty, Rachel, and Clare zoomed after Jack Frost, flying high above him as he sprinted across the park. They watched him run around the park fountain, past the friendship sign on the wall of the tennis clubhouse, and right into the tent where the Summer Friends Camp was based.

"Follow him into the tent!" called Kirsty in an urgent voice. "If we can corner him in there, maybe we can find a way to get the ring back!"

They flew toward the tent opening, but at the last second Jack Frost slapped the tent flap shut and tied it from the inside. The three fairies bounced off it and landed on the grass with a bump. Rachel glanced around quickly, but no one had seen them.

"Luckily everyone's either at the barbecue or the ice cream stand," she said, flying back up to the tent flap and whacking it. "Let us in! You can't stay in there forever!"

"Go away and bother someone else," Jack Frost called. "I like being the boss of all these new friends, and I'm not giving the ring back, no matter what you say!"

The three fairies stared at one another, and then Rachel snapped her fingers.

"I've got it!" she said. "Jack Frost loves ice cream. I bet he'd come out of the tent if we could offer him something really amazing."

"Coming right up," said Clare, waving her wand.

A large cone of ice cream suddenly appeared on the grass outside the tent, standing in its own special holder. The cone was glittering blue and the ice cream was as white as frost, with sparkling blue sauce cascading over the top.

"That is a beautiful ice cream cone," said Kirsty in a loud voice.

"It's so blue and glittery. I bet it tastes amazing."

"It's blueberry cream flavored," said Clare. "It's bursting with the taste of real, juicy blueberries and rich, smooth vanilla. The cone is made of sugar and fizzy candy."

The fairies saw the tent flap open slightly. One suspicious eye peered out at the ice cream.

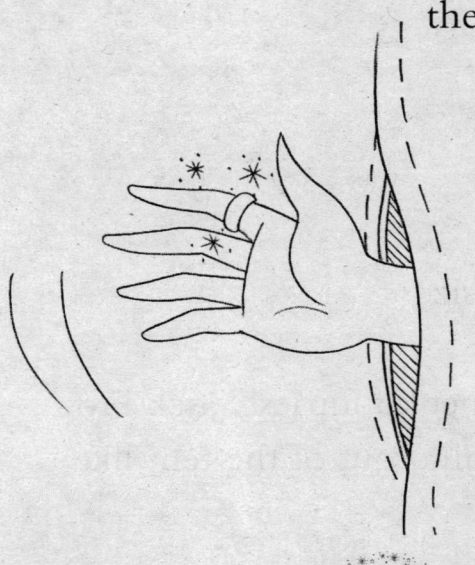

"Get ready," Rachel whispered. Suddenly, Jack Frost's hand shot out through the tent flap.

As he grabbed the ice cream, Kirsty and
Clare threw their arms around his wrist,
holding on as tightly as they could while
Rachel tugged on the ring.

Jack Frost twisted his arm and roared
with fury, but Rachel was strong and
determined. Just as Jack Frost finally
wrenched his hand
away from the
fairies, the ring
came off in
Rachel's hands.
She handed it
to Clare and it
shrank to fairy size
instantly.

"You tricky, sneaky fairies!" Jack Frost
screeched, charging out of the tent like
an angry bull.

"We were only taking back what belongs to Clare," said Kirsty, joining hands with Rachel and Clare. "You obviously don't know very much about true friends."

"Oh, yes I do," said Jack Frost in an offended voice. "I just made lots of new friends. They all want to do nice things for me. They just went to get me some ice cream."

He looked down at the ice cream in his hand and gave it a big lick.

"But friendship isn't about giving orders," said Rachel. "You can't just boss your friends around and expect to get your own way all the time."

Jack Frost's mouth fell open in surprise. "Why not?" he demanded.

"Because *everyone's* feelings are important," said Clare. "Not just yours. True friends care about and are kind to one another. That's what real friendship is."

"Real friendship is about always having someone standing beside you, ready to help," Kirsty added.

Jack Frost took another lick of his ice

cream. He looked very thoughtful.

"I like the sound of that," he said in a quiet voice. "I wish I had some real friends."

He gobbled down the rest of his ice cream. Rachel, Kirsty, and Clare exchanged surprised glances.

"This doesn't sound like Jack Frost!" said Rachel.

"It's a pity my plan didn't work," Jack Frost went on. "I liked having humans waiting on me hand and foot. But now that I know the secret, I'm going to be the best friend of all time!"

"What do you mean?" Clare asked.

Something strange was happening to Jack Frost's face. It was something that Rachel and Kirsty had never seen before.

"He's *smiling*," Kirsty whispered, hardly able to believe her eyes. "He's actually smiling a real smile—a caring smile!"

"I'm going to throw a party," said Jack Frost, rubbing his hands together. "I'm going to invite all my goblin friends. And they love ice cream just as much as I do, so it'll be an ice cream party!"

The three fairies didn't know what to say. They just stared at him in amazement. They had never heard him being so friendly.

"Do you like ice cream, too?" he asked.

They nodded, and Jack Frost opened his arms wide.

"Then you are all invited—along with the other Friendship Fairies, of course. Let's have a party to celebrate real friendship!"

Clare still seemed to be too surprised
to move, but Rachel and Kirsty fluttered
forward, smiling.

"We'd love to come," they said.

Jack Frost grinned and disappeared
with a flash of blue lightning.

Laughing in surprise and delight, Clare
lifted her wand. Rachel and Kirsty saw
her mood ring glittering on her finger.

"Come on, let's go to Fairyland and
find the other Friendship Fairies," Clare
said. "We have a party to attend!"

A Surprising Party

The party at the Ice Castle was in full
swing by the time Rachel and Kirsty
arrived with the Friendship Fairies.
The castle door was wide open, and
glittering blue lights adorned every
turret. Arm in arm, the girls fluttered in
with Esther, Mary, Mimi, and Clare.
Florence the Friendship Fairy was close
behind them.

The Gobolicious Band was playing a lively tune, and there were tables set up all around the courtyard for guests to make their own ice cream sundaes. Huge bowls were scattered around the tables, filled with every flavor of ice cream that Rachel and Kirsty could imagine. Some goblins were dancing and some were squawking at one another, but most were making tall sundaes and gobbling them up as fast as they could.

Jack Frost spotted the fairies and came hurrying through the crowd of guests.

"Welcome to my party!" he said, beaming. "What kind of ice cream would you like?"

He scooped ice cream for them all and led them toward the tables.

"Come over here," he said. "Make

sundaes and eat them, and then come
dance, all right?"

Rachel and Kirsty couldn't help but
smile as he turned to greet the next
guests. Even though he sounded bossy,
they knew that Jack Frost was trying his
best to be a good host.

"How are you?" they heard him
demanding of a small goblin. "Tell

me your favorite flavor of ice cream. Quickly!"

"It's amazing," said Rachel. "Jack Frost is really trying hard to be a caring friend."

"I guess Clare's mood ring worked its magic on him without him knowing it," said Kirsty.

Side by side, they created glorious ice-cream sundaes in a rainbow of colors, topped with sprinkles of nuts.

"We can't thank you enough for all of your help," said Clare as they all dug into their ice cream with long spoons.

"We could never have imagined that our adventures would end with a party here in the Ice Castle!" Mimi added. "It's all thanks to you."

"We care about all our fairy friends,"

said Kirsty. "We just want you to be happy."

Esther and Mary stepped forward and gave each of the girls a tiny silver charm. Each was shaped like a fairy in mid-flight.

"They are to add to your friendship bracelets," Esther explained.

"They're to show that you are best friends to all the fairies," Mary added.

Thrilled, the girls slipped the charms into their pockets and hugged the fairies.

"We've had a lot of fun," said Rachel. "I hope we'll see you again soon."

"True friends are always together in their hearts," said Florence.

Smiling, Florence raised her wand and the world seemed to shimmer around them. Sparkling fairy dust lifted Rachel and Kirsty into the air. They blinked, and found that they were standing in Rainspell Park, close to the barbecue party. The sound of laughter and happy conversation filled the air.

"There you are, girls," called Mr. Walker. "I'm just going to get some more burgers so that everyone can have one."

"OK, Dad," said Rachel, giving him a big smile.

Everything was back to normal. Oscar and Lara came running toward them, hand in hand.

"Look what we made together," said Lara.

Oscar held out two badges with "Summer Friends Camp" printed on them.

"They're special badges for everyone at the camp," said Oscar. "And we were hoping that you both might agree to be pen pals with us, so we can stay friends after we leave the island."

"We don't want to lose touch with the wonderful new friends we've made," Lara added.

"We'd love to," said Rachel and Kirsty together.

Just then, Jen stepped up onto a hay bale and motioned for the crowd to quiet down. Ginny stood at her side.

"We're absolutely delighted to see so many of our friends here today," said Jen, gazing around at the crowd. "Thank you for coming."

"We've really enjoyed running the Summer Friends Camp together," Ginny went on. "We've made lots of new friends and had tons of fun along the way. We thought that we would be teaching you, but actually *you* have taught *us* the meaning of friendship."

"We care about each and every one of you," Jen continued. "We will never forget our amazing summer, and we hope that you will be back on Rainspell again next year."

"We can't wait!" Ginny finished.

There was a roar of applause, and the teenage best friends stepped down from the hay bale. Rachel and Kirsty ran over to them.

"That was an awesome speech," said Rachel.

Jen and Ginny hugged them.

"You two are amazing," said Jen. "You're such a fantastic example of a true friendship. I've never seen you get angry with each other."

"And you always listen to each other's point of view," Ginny added. "We're going to try to be more like you in the future."

Rachel and Kirsty felt a little bit embarrassed, but very pleased. They shared a secret, happy smile and linked their little fingers together.

"I'm so happy that I met you here on Rainspell," Kirsty said. "Isn't it wonderful that we've been best friends ever since?"

"And that won't ever change," said Rachel, smiling. "Best friends forever!"

RAINBOW magic

SPECIAL EDITION

Rachel and Kirsty have found the
Friendship Fairies' missing magic items.
Now it's time for them to help

Carmen
the Cheerleading Fairy!

Join their next adventure in this
special sneak peek . . .

Perilous Practice

"I can't believe we're finally here!" Kirsty Tate cried, grinning. "I've always dreamed about taking part in a real cheerleading competition."

Her best friend, Rachel Walker,

squeezed her hand. "I can believe it!
You and your squad have worked really
hard. I'm so glad I got to come along to
watch you compete!"

The girls linked arms and skipped
across the huge lawn in the middle of the
Cove College campus. They'd come to
Cove City with Kirsty's parents for the
big Junior Cheerleading Competition
that weekend! It was Kirsty's first year on
a squad, and this was their very first
competition. Rachel and Kirsty had only
just arrived, but the weekend already felt
magical!

"Tumble over that way!" Mr. Tate
called from behind the girls, pointing to a
large brick building on one corner of the
lawn. The archway over the door read
COVE COLLEGE GYMNASIUM.

Kirsty smiled and did a series of cartwheels on her way to the gym. Rachel whooped and applauded as Mr. and Mrs. Tate caught up with them.

"Is the rest of your squad meeting you here?" Rachel asked, pulling the gym door open.

"Yup! It's our last practice before the competition tomorrow," Kirsty said, peering around the massive gym in awe. "Though I'm not sure how I'll ever find them. This place is huge!"

Girls and boys were scattered all over the gym. Some were stretching and warming up, while others chatted excitedly. Colorful mats covered the floor, and Rachel and Kirsty could see piles of pom-poms and stacks of megaphones over by the bleachers.

"Kirsty!" a voice suddenly called. A girl with a curly black ponytail ran up and gave Kirsty a hug. "Can you believe all this?"

Kirsty shook her head, smiling. "I guess we need a big gym to hold this much cheer!" She turned to Rachel. "Rachel, this is my friend Sunny. She's the captain of our squad."

"I can't wait to see your routine!" Rachel said, waving as Kirsty and Sunny ran off to join their teammates.

"Come on, Rachel," Mrs. Tate said. "Let's find a spot on the bleachers to watch them practice."

From the bleachers, Rachel, Mr. Tate, and Mrs. Tate had a perfect view of the whole gym. There was an awful lot to see! Rachel counted ten different squads

practicing before she turned her attention back to Kirsty's team.

"Okay, let's go!" Sunny cried. She and a boy with spiky brown hair led the squad in their opening cheer. Rachel couldn't help noticing that they were all out of sync—some of the kids were forgetting the words, and others were doing the wrong arm movements. *Maybe they just need a minute to get warmed up*, Rachel thought, frowning.

Their coach, Mrs. Gold, stood to one side, shaking her head in confusion.

"I've never seen them make so many mistakes," Mrs. Tate murmured. "What could be going on?"

RAINBOW magic™
SPECIAL EDITION

Which Magical Fairies Have You Met?

- ❏ Joy the Summer Vacation Fairy
- ❏ Holly the Christmas Fairy
- ❏ Kylie the Carnival Fairy
- ❏ Stella the Star Fairy
- ❏ Shannon the Ocean Fairy
- ❏ Trixie the Halloween Fairy
- ❏ Gabriella the Snow Kingdom Fairy
- ❏ Juliet the Valentine Fairy
- ❏ Mia the Bridesmaid Fairy
- ❏ Flora the Dress-Up Fairy
- ❏ Paige the Christmas Play Fairy
- ❏ Emma the Easter Fairy
- ❏ Cara the Camp Fairy
- ❏ Destiny the Rock Star Fairy
- ❏ Belle the Birthday Fairy
- ❏ Olympia the Games Fairy
- ❏ Selena the Sleepover Fairy

- ❏ Cheryl the Christmas Tree Fairy
- ❏ Florence the Friendship Fairy
- ❏ Lindsay the Luck Fairy
- ❏ Brianna the Tooth Fairy
- ❏ Autumn the Falling Leaves Fairy
- ❏ Keira the Movie Star Fairy
- ❏ Addison the April Fool's Day Fairy
- ❏ Bailey the Babysitter Fairy
- ❏ Natalie the Christmas Stocking Fairy
- ❏ Lila and Myla the Twins Fairies
- ❏ Chelsea the Congratulations Fairy
- ❏ Carly the School Fairy
- ❏ Angelica the Angel Fairy
- ❏ Blossom the Flower Girl Fairy
- ❏ Skyler the Fireworks Fairy
- ❏ Giselle the Christmas Ballet Fairy
- ❏ Alicia the Snow Queen Fairy

31901063824769

SCHOLASTIC

Find all of your favorite fairy friends at
scholastic.com/rainbowmagic

3 stories in each one!

HIT entertainment

RMSPECIAL20